Galia Bernstein

I AM A CAT

Peachtree

Abrams Books for Young Readers

New York

"Hello, my name is Simon.

I am a cat. Just like you!"

"A cat?" said Lion. "Don't be silly, dear boy. You can't be a cat because I am a cat, and you are nothing like me at all. Cats have a mane and a tuft at the end of their tails, and when they roar everybody trembles for they are the kings of all beasts!"

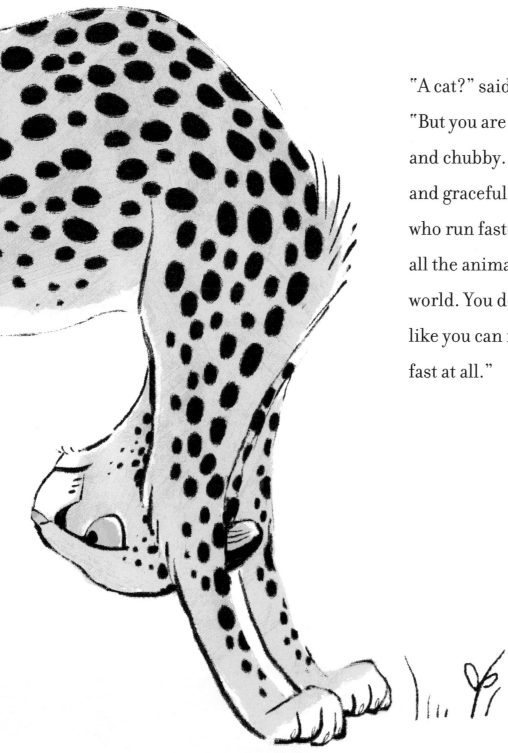

"A cat?" said Cheetah. "But you are so short and chubby. Cats are tall and graceful creatures who run faster than all the animals in the world. You don't look like you can run very fast at all."

"A cat?" said Puma. "That's ridiculous! Cats live in the mountains—that's why people call us Mountain Lions. They leap far, jump high, and act tough! I know fuzzy little rabbits that look tougher than you."

"A cat? Cats are black," said Panther. "They live in jungles and rain forests and sleep in trees. Have you ever even seen a jungle?"

"A cat?" said Tiger. "That's very funny. You see, cats are very big and very strong and very, very orange. You are small and gray. You might be some kind of rat, but a cat? I don't think so."

Simon was confused. "Lion is the only one with a mane," he said. "No one else is black like Panther or orange like Tiger. No one else can jump as high as Puma or can run as fast as Cheetah. So how can you all be cats?"

"Because we also have many things in common," said Lion. "We all have small, perky ears and flat noses . . . "

" . . . long whiskers and long tails."

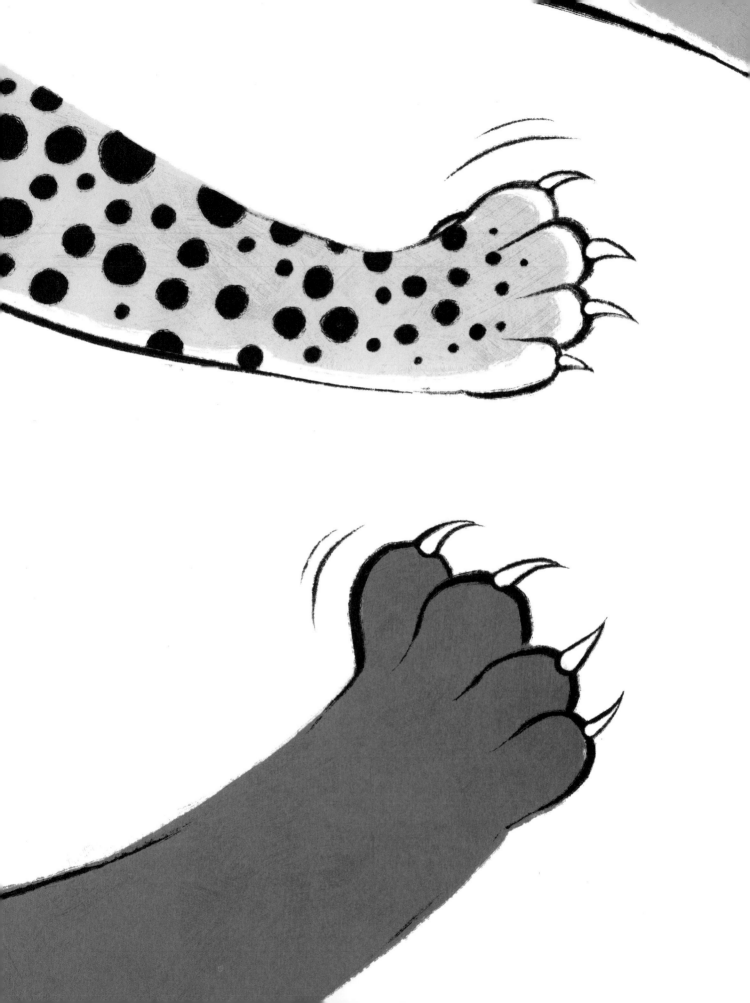

"We have sharp teeth and claws . . . ”

" . . . and big eyes that can see in the dark."

"So do I," said Simon.

"I have all of those things."

"Only smaller."

They all leaned in
for a closer look.

Ah... said Lion.

Oh...
said Puma.

Um...

"In that case . . ." said Panther.

Er...

"It's very possible that . . ."
said Tiger.

You're a cat!

said Cheetah.

"So, I'm part of the family?"

asked Simon.

The big cats looked at one another.

"YES!" they all said together.

And they spent the rest of the day pouncing
and prowling, prancing and playing, like
cats of all sizes do.

To Sheera and Haddar,
my small but fearless first critics.

The art for this book was created digitally with applied hand-painted textures.

Cataloging-in-Publication Data has been applied for and may be obtained from the Library of Congress.
ISBN: 978-1-4197-2643-9

Text and illustrations copyright © 2017 Galia Bernstein
Book design by Pamela Notarantonio

Printed and bound in U.S.A.
12 11 10 9 8 7 6 5 4 3

Abrams Books for Young Readers are available at special discounts when purchased in quantity for premiums and promotions as well as fundraising or educational use. Special editions can also be created to specification. For details, contact specialsales@abramsbooks.com or the address below.

ABRAMS The Art of Books
195 Broadway, New York, NY 10007
abramsbooks.com